Mr. Groundhog
WANTS THE DAY OFF

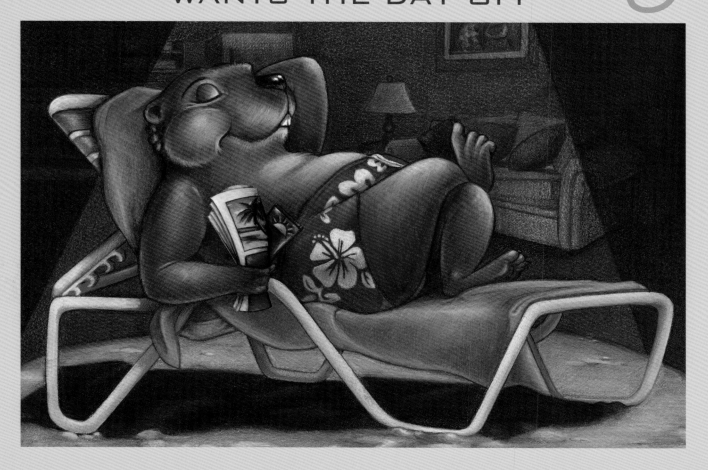

WRITTEN BY

Pat Stemper Vojta Olga Levitskiy

ILLUSTRATED BY

Thanks to my husband Ken for his support, and the joys of my life, Charlie, Nathan and Roxanne, who continue to make me a proud parent, and also Cassi for sharing this journey. ❧ With love, P.V.

To my family, with love and appreciation ❧ O.L.

Text ©2010 by Pat Stemper Vojta
Illustration ©2010 by Olga Levitskiy

Vojta, Pat Stemper.

    Mr. Groundhog wants the day off / written by Pat Stemper Vojta;
    illustrated by Olga Levitskiy—1 ed. —McHenry, IL : Raven Tree Press, 2010.

    p.;cm.

    SUMMARY: Mr. Groundhog is tired of everyone blaming him for six more
              weeks of winter. He asks all of his friends to take over for the day.

English-only Edition
ISBN 978-1-934960-79-0 hardcover

Bilingual Edition
ISBN 978-1-934960-77-6 hardcover
ISBN 978-1-934960-78-3 paperback

    Audience: pre-K to 3rd grade
    Title available in English-only or bilingual English-Spanish editions

    1. Holidays & Celebrations/Other—Juvenile fiction. 2. Animals/Mammals—Juvenile fiction.
    I. Illust. Levitskiy, Olga. II. Title.

LCCN: 2009931227

Printed in Taiwan
10 9 8 7 6 5 4 3 2 1
First Edition

Free activities for this book are available at www.raventreepress.com

Raven Tree Press
A Division of Delta Systems Co., Inc.
www.raventreepress.com

PRINTED WITH
SOY INK

"I will not do Groundhog Day anymore!" said Mr. Groundhog.
"I'm tired of everyone getting mad at me!
They see my shadow and blame me for six more weeks of winter.
I quit!"

Mr. Groundhog stood next to the hole in the ground where he lived in the park.
Everyone would wait there to see him on Groundhog Day.
He jogged around the park to help him think.

He stopped fast when he saw he was nose–to–nose with Mrs. Rabbit.
"Oh, hello, Mrs. Rabbit," said Mr. Groundhog. Mrs. Rabbit smiled.
"Will you do Groundhog Day for me this year?" asked Mr. Groundhog.
"I'm sorry, I can't. I'm much too busy getting ready for Easter.
I have eggs to color and I must practice the Bunny Hop to lead
the parade. But I have something for you."

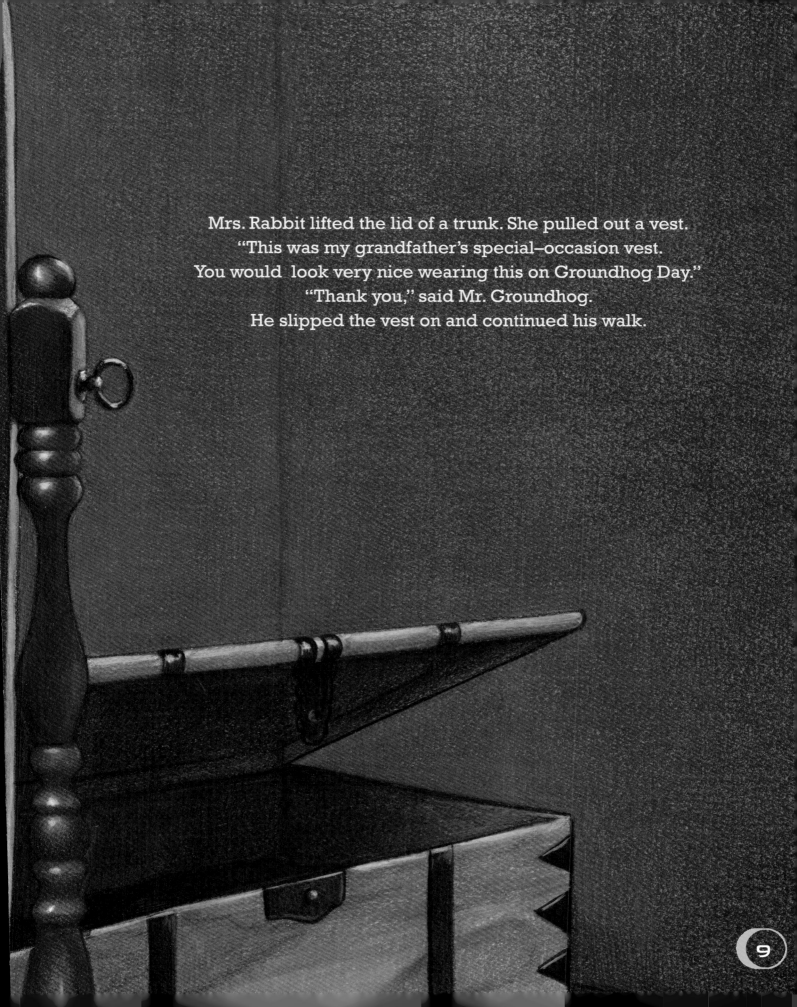

Mrs. Rabbit lifted the lid of a trunk. She pulled out a vest.
"This was my grandfather's special—occasion vest.
You would look very nice wearing this on Groundhog Day."
"Thank you," said Mr. Groundhog.
He slipped the vest on and continued his walk.

Then he met Mr. Turtle.

"Hi, Mr. Turtle. Would you mind doing Groundhog Day for me?" asked Mr. Groundhog.
"All you have to do is come out and greet the crowd of people."
"I would, but I can't fit into that small opening of your home.
My shell would get stuck," explained Mr. Turtle. "But I have something for you."

Mr. Groundhog followed Mr. Turtle to a cluster of bushes.
Mr. Turtle reached in and lifted out a hat.
"This is my holiday hat.
I want you to wear it on Groundhog Day," said Mr. Turtle.

"Thank you," Mr. Groundhog said as he put on the hat.
Next, he saw Mrs. Squirrel. "Mrs. Squirrel, will you do Groundhog Day for me?"
"I am really sorry, but I would be too afraid to go down into that dark hole
to get to your home. But I have something for you," said Mrs. Squirrel.

She reached up and broke some branches off a tree.
"You can use one of these for a cane. It will look nice with your vest and hat."
"Thank you," said Mr. Groundhog as he hooked the branch around his arm.

As Mr. Groundhog walked back home, he met Mrs. Raccoon.
"Mr. Groundhog, you look very handsome. I have something for you," said Mrs. Raccoon.
She took a piece of ribbon off her head and tied it around Mr. Groundhog's neck.

"Thank you," said Mr. Groundhog.
The next morning, sunlight woke the sleeping groundhog.
Mr. Groundhog got up and hurried into his outfit.

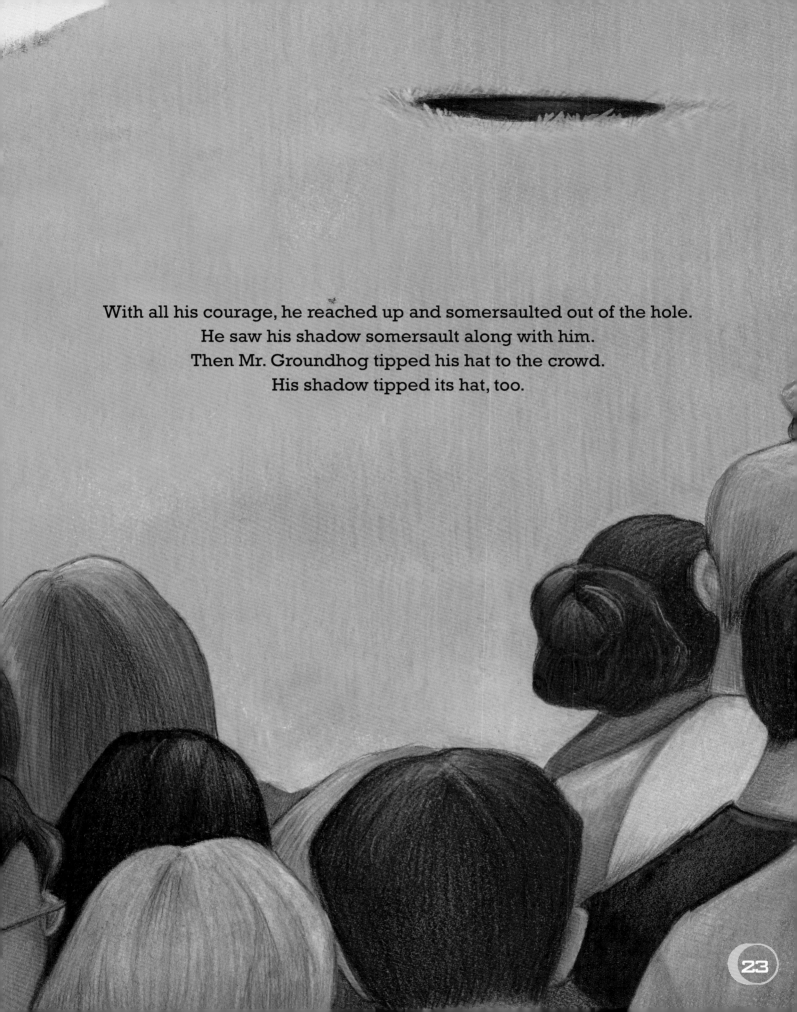

With all his courage, he reached up and somersaulted out of the hole.
He saw his shadow somersault along with him.
Then Mr. Groundhog tipped his hat to the crowd.
His shadow tipped its hat, too.

The band began to play.
Mr. Groundhog reached out his arms and began to dance.
His shadow danced, too.

Mr. Turtle looked at the ground and saw that he had a shadow.
He began to dance. His shadow danced, too.
Mrs. Squirrel joined in. Soon everyone was dancing.

"I never knew how much fun a shadow could be," said Mrs. Squirrel.
"I'm looking forward to next Groundhog Day."

Mr. Groundhog was happy.
He smiled at his shadow and said, "Thank you, my friend.
I'll see you again the next sunny day."